HOWLING *for* FLAME

CAROLINE MALTSEV

HOWLING *for* FLAME

TATE PUBLISHING
AND **ENTERPRISES,** LLC

Published by Tate Publishing & Enterprises, LLC
127 E. Trade Center Terrace | Mustang, Oklahoma 73064 USA
1.888.361.9473 | www.tatepublishing.com

Tate Publishing is committed to excellence in the publishing industry. The company reflects the philosophy established by the founders, based on Psalm 68:11,
"The Lord gave the word and great was the company of those who published it."

Book design copyright © 2012 by Tate Publishing, LLC. All rights reserved.
Cover design by Errol Villamante
Interior design by Joana Quilantang

Published in the United States of America

ISBN: 978-1-62147-189-9

1. Fiction / Coming of Age
2. Fiction / Action & Adventure
12.08.27

ACKNOWLEDGMENTS

I want to thank my mom, who always kept pushing me to write my book; my dad, who always listened to my ideas as we were driving in the car; my stepmom Lyuda, who helped me with figuring out what to do with the book and always supporting my ideas, my stepsister, Katya, who helped me a lot with cover page design; my cousin, Mark, and my grandmother, Irene, for reading the rough drafts; to Kendall S. for reading it beyond countless times and always telling me her honest opinion; to Kelly H. for support; Mrs. Reed, who gave me my first Harry Potter book and made me realize how much I really loved fantasy books; and, of course, my fifth grade English teacher, Mrs. Cooper, my sixth grade English teacher, Mr. J. Waller, and my sixth grade reading teacher, Mrs. Mulligan, who always supported my writing and told me how to improve. Also, though they do not know it, to the many authors whose books I have read. They have inspired me to write my own book and widen my imagination.

CONTENTS

Acknowledgments 5

Chapter 1.. 7

Chapter 2.. 14

Chapter 3.. 19

Chapter 4.. 21

Chapter 5.. 25

Chapter 6.. 35

Chapter 7.. 44

Chapter 8.. 53

Chapter 9.. 58

Chapter 10.. 67

Chapter 11.. 73

Chapter 12.. 80

Chapter 13.. 91

Chapter 14.. 95

Chapter 15.. 103

Chapter 16.. 106

CHAPTER 1

I was running. The guards were about thirty meters behind me, but they were all on horses. I ran into the forest, holding the satchel tightly next to my side. I stopped and rested behind a thick tree. I heard the horses neigh as they tried to get into the forest, but realized they couldn't. This forest, the forest I named The Dark Forest because of the many trees blocking out the sun, making it hard to see even by day, was one of the forests that horses can't go in because of the thick trees and how close they are.

I held my breath and waited for the guards' reactions.

"God, not again!" shouted the boss of the guards. "I can't believe we let him get away again!"

Him? I thought. *Why do people always think that thieves are boys or men? Well, they usually are, but I'm an exception. And anyways, I make a pretty good thief for a girl.*

"So what do we do now?" asked one of the guards.

"He'll be coming in next week, market day is on Wednesday. I think we can afford to give him a week's head start," answered the boss. I heard the horses trot away. I looked in the satchel to see if I had all the money, and thank God I did.

I took off my mask and started walking toward the campsite, deep inside The Dark Forest. There was no direct path to the campsite. You could only get there if you knew how, which was to read the markings on the trees. We used our knives to make carvings in the trees which would lead us to camp. To any passerby, they would look like animal's markings, but to us, it was the path to our hideout.

I followed the path I had come to know so well, even though I had only been with the thieves for about five weeks. It takes about ten minutes if you can avoid obstacles, but I was so tired from running that it took me about twenty minutes to get to the campsite. When I finally did get to the campsite, some of the thieves were sitting by a fire.

"What took you so long?" demanded the top thief, Virp.

Towering over everyone else in the group, Virp seemed like he could shatter anyone's body. His maroon eyes matched his hair and his face reddened because of my lateness.

I dropped the satchel in front of him. "Guards," I answered simply. "Some woman saw me pickpocket a man and she started to yell her head off, but I still got the wallet and got out of there."

"How far did the guards follow you this time?" asked Virp.

"Only to the beginning of the forest. They gave up once they found out their horses couldn't go through the trees. They expect me to come on market day again. The boss guard said that they can afford to give me a week's head start."

"Reasonable," said Virp. "Do they still think you're a boy?"

"Yes. And if the woman said that it was a girl they probably wouldn't believe her. People don't think that girls can be thieves."

"Yes, well, they are rather wrong, aren't they?" said Virp. He picked up the satchel and started to count the money.

I took a look at the rest of the men and boys sitting around the fire.

Not everyone in the group was there, they were probably out somewhere stealing or making deals with other thieves, but the ones I knew the most were sitting around the fire. Three men and two boys were lounging on logs, talking and laughing. Mano, the next in line after Virp, was telling a joke, keeping everyone in suspense of what he was about to say next. His dark black hair swayed as he moved his head while telling his joke, and the fire reflected in his brown eyes.

Kato, the shortest man in the group, was sitting across from Mano, his back towards me. His hunched back gave an impression that he was an old man when he really wasn't. He turned around for second and locked eyes with me, his penetrating blue ones making me squirm. After a moment, he turned back around, running his hand over his short brown hair that was always cut close to his head.

Milano was sitting the furthest away from the fire, sharpening his knives and looking bored. Even though he was the older than anyone here, he was still able to do anything a healthy twenty year old man could do, including killing something. Although I could definitely outrun him, he could track me down and kill me. Manka was one of the two boys around the fire. He was eagerly listening to Mano telling his joke, as if each word could one day save his life. He was constantly brushing his long brown hair out of his face, where, for a minute or so, you could see his eyes which were a colored imitation of his hair, before his bangs covered them again. Deso was the other boy in the group and he stood out the most. Where the others had brown or black hair, Deso's hair was as golden as the sun, with sky-blue eyes.

As Mano finished his joke, everyone but Milano roared with laughter. Milano simply scoffed and proceeded sharpening his knives. After the laughter died down, Deso commented on something and the men laughed some more. Deso looked over at me and winked.

"Not bad, not bad," Virp said, tossing the satchel of money onto a log by the fire. "This can keep us busy for a little while."

"Good. Make it count because I can't go into town until I get a new mask," I said. I walked into my tent, which I awkwardly shared with the boys and sat down on a blanket.

"Hey, can you patch this up for me? It ripped when I was getting more wood for the fire." Deso had walked in and was holding a pair of old pants that had a giant hole on the side of them.

"Sure. Hand them over," I replied. I took a sewing kit from underneath my pillow and started to sew it.

"Sooo...where you from?" asked Deso.

"I don't do background stories, Deso."

Deso brushed his hair out of his face. "Why not?" he asked.

I shrugged. "Too depressing?"

"You tell me yours and I'll tell you mine," Deso offered.

"All right. I grew up with my mom and dad. Dad died in a war, and Mom died from depression. Before she did, I had to do everything, including force-feed her. She just seemed like she didn't have the will to live anymore. And when she finally died, I had to go to an orphanage. I was only eight. I was there for four years. Nobody wanted me so I ran away. Then, I was walking through the woods and... you know what happened next."

Deso smiled. "I do," he said. "I was afraid that Virp was going to kill you."

"*You* were afraid?" I asked.

"Well, you didn't look very afraid."

"Good." He looked at me questionably, but I kept busy with the sewing.

"So how do you know how to sew?" he asked.

"Mom and I used to sew together when Dad messed his clothes up. And I helped the nuns at the orphanage."

"Interesting."

"Your turn," I said.

He sighed. "Well, unlike you, I didn't have a family, at least not one that I can remember. I grew up in an orphanage. Then, one day, I was in town with one of the nuns and I saw Virp pick pocketing a man on the street. Someone called the guards and I decided that I could stop him so I followed him. No one knew I left and Virp only discovered me when he was deep inside the forest. I put on my best please-don't-kill-me-today-I-can-have-some-use-for-you look and he took me into the family. Plus, I knew how to steal things without being caught, but Virp taught me better."

"How old were you when you followed him?" I asked.

"Seven, I think."

We sat in silence for a while and I sewed his pants. After about ten minutes, Manka popped his head in.

"Food," he said. The magic word. Deso and I rushed up and went to the campfire.

"Here's to the girl who brought us enough money to survive for two weeks!" cried Virp, holding his mug in a toast for me. All of the thieves cheered and slammed their mugs into the others. Deso and Manka patted my back. We had some meat and some water, and went on our way so we wouldn't be hurt when the rest of the thieves got drunk. Virp always said beer was too precious to let kids drink. Back in the tent, we joked and laughed the night away and listened to the drunken men sing their songs and drink their beer.

CHAPTER 2

The tent we slept in was small but roomy. Since there was no floor but there was ground, one big blanket covered the land and we all got our separate blankets. I slept in the middle of Deso and Manka because the first night I came into the possession of Virp, I was scared and they comforted me.

I woke up the next morning to find Deso facing me, with his arm around my waist and his other arm under my head. I quickly got up and saw that, thankfully, Manka was still sleeping. I went outside and found most of the men on the logs sleeping with the mugs still in their hands. I chuckled to myself and wrapped my arms around me. Fall was definitely coming and we all needed more clothes, which meant we needed to steal more.

I walked a little farther into the woods where the river was. Before washing my face, I looked into my reflection. My sea-green, almond-shaped eyes twinkled back at me, and my golden-brown hair slid down my back as I let it out of its braid. I tucked my hair behind my ear and sprayed the cool, blue, crystal gems on my face. I dried my face with my shirt, and after realizing it was dirty, remembered that today was my day to wash the clothes.

I headed back to the campsite and started a fire and breakfast. I was usually up the earliest and it wasn't that hard to make breakfast, in my case. After the men found out I could cook a breakfast without burning it, they fully accepted me into their group.

The smell of meat woke up Deso, who came out of the tent looking refreshed.

He ruffled his golden hair and asked, "How'd you sleep?"

I remembered the way I woke up that morning and blushed. "Fine," I answered. "And you?"

Deso looked pleased with himself. "Pretty well, thank you."

"Why do you look so smug?" I asked.

He shot me a sly smile. "Oh, nothing. Just...got a lot of rest."

I ignored him and continued making breakfast.

"Good morning!" Manka said, coming out of the tent.

I chuckled. "Someone slept well," I said.

"You bet I did!" Manka answered. Pretty soon the smell of meat woke the men up and they gathered around the fire, waiting for their serve.

When we were all eating I said, "Virp, we're going to need new clothes. Winter is coming soon and we need jackets."

"That's true," grumbled Virp. "Kato, go down to the village in a couple of days and buy clothes for all of us, especially jackets."

Kato mumbled under his breath but didn't object further.

"And you three," Virp said, pointing to us kids, "you need to go to town and pickpocket some people. We could use some money."

"I just brought you a whole satchel full of wallets yesterday!" I argued.

"We need more for jackets and shoes and such. We don't have enough."

"There's at least seventy dollars in there!"

"Didn't you hear me?" snarled Virp. "I said we need more money!" He punched the log he was sitting on, making pieces of wood fly everywhere.

"Fine." I sighed. I was the only one who would dare talk back to Virp.

After breakfast, I had to wash all the clothes, which was disturbing after the men were drunk last night. After that, Deso, Manka, and I went into town to get some money. Instead of pick pocketing, though, we decided to steal from a store.

"Here's how it's going to work," I instructed, "I'll distract the owner by asking him questions about something. You guys go through the store and take stuff from the shelves.

We go in like we don't know each other and that's how we walk out. Don't look at each other, okay?" They nodded. "Okay, let's go," I said.

I went in first and started to ask the owner how much a lot of things cost. Meanwhile, Deso and Manka came in one at a time, stealing things and putting them in their pockets very casually.

Very nice, I thought.

I left after about five minutes, apologizing to the owner that there wasn't anything I could buy for my mom, which wasn't exactly a lie. I went to the center of the town and waited. After about ten minutes, Deso and Manka walked toward me with huge smiles on their faces.

"Okay, let's go before we get caught," I said. The boys nodded and we went toward the forest. When we finally got to the campsite, we showed Virp the things we stole, and even he was impressed.

"Kato! Come here!" shouted Virp. Kato walked over. "See these? Take these to the market and sell them. Get the money, buy us clothes, and come back."

"But don't go to Oliver's store," I warned him. "That's where we got the stuff from."

Kato nodded, took the items, and left.

"Good job, Deso, Manka, and Flame," said Virp. Then he went into his tent.

Deso looked at me. "Flame?" he asked. "That's your name?"

I looked at the ground. "Well...yes. I don't remember my real name and the first night that I came here I was pretty mad and feisty so he decided to name me Flame because flames are uncontrollable."

"Oh...well, I think it's nice," he said.

"Thanks," I replied. Deso walked away and when I looked at Manka he was making a heart with his hands as if he was seeing me and Deso in love.

I shoved him. "Stop!" I said. "It's not going to happen!"

Manka laughed and walked away. I followed the path Deso had just walked on seconds before with my eyes. I shook my head and went into the tent to sleep. I didn't feel like eating so I just fell asleep.

CHAPTER 3

I woke up the next morning feeling refreshed. Manka and Deso were already out of the tent. I walked out to the fire to see that Deso was trying to make breakfast and smoke was coming out of the chicken. I rushed over to help him.

"Flip the chicken over, the first side is done," I told him. He did as I asked, but not without burning his fingers. I took the pot from him and cooked the breakfast. After breakfast, Virp came over to the three of us, saying that we needed to steal even more items. He handed me the satchel.

"You guys need to get a lot of stuff. We need a lot of money," he said. "But don't hit every place at once. Steal some things from a store, hide out a little in the town's center, and then hit another store. Don't get caught. If you're not here before sundown, we're going to move our location without you. Got it?"

Virp pushed us toward the entrance, or, in our case, the exit of the forest. We got to the town's center and we did exactly as Virp said. We stole things from a store and then hid out in the town's center for an hour, and then we stole again. When the sky started to turn pink we decided to head back. By the time we got to the campsite it was still light, but everyone had already moved!

"Where'd they go?" asked Manka.

"They lied!" Deso exclaimed.

"We were here before sundown though!" Manka shouted.

While those two were being mad about the thieves leaving us, I looked closer to the trees. Pieces of meat were strapped onto them.

"Guys," I said, "we have to get out of here."

"Why?" asked Manka.

"They didn't leave pieces of meat strapped to trees by accident. Don't wolves hunt at night?" I asked.

"Yes…what about wolves?" asked Manka.

"I think they left us here to die. The wolves are going to come soon. They can smell meat. We need to get someplace high, like in a tree."

"I don't think they would do that…you know Virp. He probably—" A howl pierced our ears. The wolves were coming.

CHAPTER 4

"Okay, we've got about ten seconds before they come," I said. "Do you guys have your knives with you?" They nodded and pulled them out of a pocket I sewed for them especially for their knives.

"Good. Don't try to kill the wolves, just harm them enough so they won't follow us."

Pretty soon, we heard another howl and then the sound of paws running through the forest. We made a circle, back to back, with our knives drawn, waiting for the attack. The wolves came in a bigger circle surrounding us.

"Are you guys ready?" I whispered.

"No," they both answered.

The first wolf lunged. It was an epic battle where there could be so many wrongs. We had to split up and I was so scared for Manka and Deso. I had quickly slit all of the wolves that were fighting me. Then, I heard a blood-curdling scream. I turned around to see that one of the wolves bit Deso around his waist. I cringed as I saw the blood flow freely from his body.

I rushed over to him and killed the wolf that had bitten him. When I turned around, Deso was on the ground bleeding. Manka and I quickly killed the rest of the wolves and then turned our attention to Deso. Letting the wolves live wouldn't be an option because they could follow the smell of blood.

"Deso!" Manka cried when he saw how badly Deso was bleeding.

"I'm...ugh...fine," Deso grunted.

"What do we do, what do we do?" Manka yelled. I took a deep breath.

"Give me your shirt," I said.

"What?" asked Manka.

"Give me your shirt!" I repeated.

Confused, Manka took off his shirt. I ripped it into long strips and tied the shirt around Deso's waist. I took some strips and ran to the river. I dipped the ripped shirt in the cool water and ran back and tied it around Deso's waist. Deso groaned with pain as I tied it around him.

"Sorry," I said. When I finished tying him, Manka and I helped him up. He perched up against a tree. I looked around some more and saw a pile of ash in one spot—the spot where our tent used to be, the spot where my sewing kit from my mother used to lay. Hate filled every one of my veins. It surged through me like burning venom. I went over to the ashes and went through them. I found a piece of burned cloth. My sewing kit was destroyed. I clenched a necklace around my neck. It was the necklace my father gave to my mother. And before mother died, she gave it to me.

A locket intertwined with a long gold chain hung around my neck. The outside of it was a painting of blue flowers. Once opened, there is one half of a heart on each side coming together. My thumb went over the inscription on the back of it. "Your love I hold with me forever," it said. When the necklace was winded, the most beautiful melody played. I remember I used to fall asleep to it when I was a child. I held onto it for a moment and then went back over to the boys.

"What happened?" asked Deso, struggling to keep the pain out of his voice.

"They burned our tent." My voice cracked. I cleared my throat. "You know what they mean when they burn our only place to live. We're out of their group."

"But why?" asked Manka.

"I don't know," I said. "All I know is that if I ever find them again…I will kill Virp."

We walked into the woods, trying to find shelter for the night. We thought being in a tree was probably the best thing to do. With much difficulty getting Deso up into a tree, we finally rested on one of the thick branches.

"You guys sleep," I said. "I'll keep watch."

"You sure?" Manka asked, yawning.

"Yes," I said. "Sleep."

Deso was already sleeping and Manka fell asleep soon afterward. I wanted to sleep also, but didn't have the heart to wake up either of the boys. I ended up falling asleep, my head against the tree trunk.

CHAPTER 5

I woke up in a house. A horrible stench rose to my nostrils and I nearly gagged. I sat up and looked around me.

"Ugghh! Where are we?" asked Manka who sat up next to me.

"We're in a house…cottage… something," I replied. We were in a kitchen sleeping on the floor with a blanket on top of it. A door opened and an old lady came through with a basket of berries. Her stringy grey hair reached her shoulders and her hunched back looked as though she might flip over at any second. She smiled a toothy smile when she saw me and Manka awake sitting on the blanket.

"Ah, good!" she said clapping her hands together. "You're awake! Now, come up and eat some breakfast." She pointed to an old wooden table that looked as though it would collapse under the basket of berries. Manka and I obeyed her command and sat in the chairs around the table.

"Eat," the woman said pointing to the berries. Manka and I ate about half of the berries, and then remembering to save some for Deso we left the berries alone. A groan came from Deso, signaling that he was awake.

"Deso!" I gasped, rushing over to him. "How are you?"

"In pain," he grunted. He tried to sit up but I pushed him back down.

"Your friend will be fine," said the old woman, her voice shaking as she spoke. "I redid his bandages while he was sleeping and he should be as good as new in a few days."

"Thank you," I said. Then a thought came to me. "Why did you get us out of that tree?" I asked.

The woman stared at me. "Surely you didn't think that I would let three children stay out in the woods on their own, did you? There could be snakes in that tree!"

Snakes, the one thing I didn't think of, I thought.

"Thank you," I repeated.

"It was no trouble at all!" said the woman.

Some more thoughts came to me, such as: How did you get us out of that tree? We were twenty feet up and why were you, an old woman, going through the woods at night where you could be attacked as easily as we could have been? But I decided not to ask them in case she got offended. After a couple of hours, Deso could finally sit up, and the woman allowed him to walk over to the table and eat some berries. After that, she went out again to get some food from the market. We sat in silence for a few minutes when Manka said, "I don't like this. We have to leave as soon as possible."

"What?" I said. "Do you have any idea what this woman has done for us? She was right about the snakes, you know. Plus, she helped Deso with his wounds and gave us food and shelter!"

"Yeah, but have you seen how she looks at us?" Manka argued. "She's got this crazy glint in her eye like she wants to eat us. Or use us."

"I highly doubt that," I said.

"Oh really?" challenged Manka. "Next time she looks at you, focus on her eyes and how they seem like she's up to something." And with that, the argument ended.

Manka was half right. She didn't eat us though. As soon as Deso got better, the old woman made us do work in her house. Usually, it was scrubbing the floor or doing dishes. The hardest thing to do was scrub the walls after she had finished cooking and food was splattered on the wall. She would make us clean when she left the house, which was a lot, and she expected the house to be clean by the time she got back, which was a long time considering she walked so slowly.

One day she got back and the house wasn't completely clean. We were still cleaning. She was incredibly disappointed. "Why aren't you done cleaning?" was the first thing she said as she came in through the door.

"We're trying," I said, scrubbing the floor harder and faster.

"After all I've done for you, I leave for a couple of hours expecting the house to be clean and I come home to this!" she yelled.

"We're almost done!" I fought back.

"Well almost isn't the same thing as *completely done*!"

"*Stop yelling at her*!" yelled Manka.

The woman turned around so quickly I thought she was about to topple over.

"What did you say, boy?" her voice had turned menacing, cold. Manka stood up from the floor.

"I told you to stop yelling at her."

The woman staggered over to Manka. She didn't even reach his shoulder.

"I'll tell you this one time, and one time only," said the woman. "Don't ever talk me or you will get the punishment you deserve."

Manka snorted. "Please! What could you—"

"Manka! I need your help," I interrupted. It would be better to not mess with the woman. Manka hesitated for a moment, but then he walked over to me and helped me scrub the floor.

"Now," said the woman. "I will leave for two hours, and when I come back, you three better be done cleaning and be sleeping!" She walked over to the door and slammed it behind her. As soon as she left, I gave Manka a hug.

"Thank you," I said. "But please, don't make her angry. I don't know what she could do to you."

"Flame, relax," Manka replied. "She's an old woman, what can she do to me?"

"Look what she has us doing!" I pointed out. "We're cleaning for her. And you were right; there is something wrong with her. We need to get out of here as soon as possible."

"Why don't we leave now?" suggested Deso.

"No. I have a feeling she would be able to find us," I said.

"So what do we do? Kill her? I'll do it," said Manka.

"Please don't," I begged. I can't stand it when people kill each other.

"Well then, what do we do? Wait till she dies? That might be in forever," said Deso.

"I don't know yet," I said. "But until then…Manka please don't do anything to upset her. I know she's small and probably powerless, but I don't think it's a good idea to upset her."

Manka seemed against my idea, but my begging faces were always amazing. He gave in. "Okay," he promised.

We were done cleaning within thirty minutes and we stood up and admired our work. The place practically gleamed. The pots and pans were polished, the floor shined so much that I could see my reflection as I walked. The clean windows had never let so much sunlight through, and the walls were shining brightly.

"Remember what she said?" I asked. The boys shook their heads. "She said we have to be in bed by the time she came back," I reminded them. We were all so tired that we didn't even say a word. We plopped down on the bed and fell asleep. After an hour of sleeping (according to the clock on the wall) I was woken up by hushed voices speaking. The old woman—and someone else—were talking in the back room. I could just make out the words.

"…don't like that boy with the brown hair at all!" the old woman said. "He talked back to me after I yelled at the girl for not being done with cleaning!"

"He didn't!" a younger voice said.

"Yes, he did! I only yelled at the girl because, after all, she does seem like the one to be, most likely, in charge of them! She told the boy to come over to help her just as he was about to say something to me. He thinks I'm powerless, but the girl is wise. She knows not to cross me."

The younger woman laughed silently. "As she should know, Salma," she said. "You are an amazing witch!"

A witch? I thought. *Oh. My. God. It's not possible!*

"Oh, dear Jain, it comes with experience!" chuckled Salma. "Anyways, I was thinking about turning the boy into a wolf if he speaks out of turn again."

"A wolf? But Salma, you know that means he would be stuck like that for eternity!" exclaimed Jain.

"Not necessarily," said Salma. "There would a way to turn him back and make him human again." I turned over so I could hear better.

"Do tell!" said Jain.

"Well, you know how when you turn somebody into an animal they are stuck like that forever? Not always. In the kingdom, far, far away, there lives a woman who knows how to bring people who are stuck as animals back to normal. Now, I don't know how she does it but it worked for my grandmother's grandmother's son. But it is almost impossible to find her."

"Where does she live exactly?" asked Jain.

"Well, I don't know exactly where, but I do know that people say that if you look on a map you see the king and queen's castle, yes? They say that she lives far past the castle on the edge of the woods near a pond that is said to be so shiny it makes the shiniest coin seem like dirt."

"What do they call her?" asked Jain. Her voice was quivering with excitement.

"I've heard they call her Mama Menny, but that was a while ago. I don't know if she still goes by that name."

"Is she still alive?"

"As of a week ago. Apparently she has kept herself alive for hundreds of years!"

"How does she do it?"

"Even I don't know that. I'm telling you, I think she's more magical than I am. But even if I do turn the boy into a wolf, the children would never run away."

"How can you be so sure? They seem very mischievous."

"Well, the girl has enough sense and the boys will follow her. And if they do run away I'll find them. You know I've memorized their scent," said Salma.

Our scent? I thought. *Is she some sort of wolf or something?*

"What if they try to kill you?" asked Jain. She sounded worried. Salma laughed so hard she almost woke up Deso.

"Kill me? Please, Jain, you know the only way to kill a witch like me is to either set me on fire or kill me with a piece of wood going through my left eye from one of these trees out here."

"My God, you're right! I completely forgot!"

"Yes, well, Jain, that is why you have to pay attention."

"You're right. I've made a fool of myself."

"Oh, don't be silly, Jain. You're as good as any other witch!"

"Just not as good as you."

"Don't you know it!" laughed Salma.

Their conversation continued to other subjects such as their clothes, and Jain's husband, but I kept listening in case they mentioned anything else about turning anyone of us into other animals. Finally, Jain got up from the table and started to leave, realizing that her husband would be home soon and she still needed to prepare dinner for him.

"Now, where can I find you again?" asked Salma. "You know I'm an old woman and we forget easily."

"Ah, Salma. Old but always as gifted as fifty years ago. And you know where! In the kingdom near the Cobbler's Street!"

"Ah, yes, yes! I almost forgot!" exclaimed Salma. Jain was getting nearer to the door, so I closed my eyes and pretended I was sleeping. I heard Jain stop near the door and turn around to look at us.

"You know, they don't seem so bad. The girl looks like she's very pretty. Which one did you say was giving you trouble?"

"That one." I knew Salma was pointing toward Manka.

"He doesn't seem so bad either," said Jain. "Wait, I almost forgot to ask you, Salma!"

"Yes, what is it, dear?" asked Salma.

"I heard an old tale once that people who turned into animals could go back to being human for an hour once a day! Is that true?"

"Indeed it is, my dear Jain."

"How do they do it?"

"They have to concentrate hard on being themselves again, but they can only stay a human for an hour a day because of the curse. Even if they try to stay in their human form longer, the will of becoming an animal becomes too strong and they turn back into one."

"Amazing!" whispered Jain. "Well, thank you, Salma, I enjoyed being here."

"My pleasure, dear Jain! You know you're welcome anytime."

With a few last good-byes and thank yous, Jain left. I pretended to sleep until the boys woke up. They shook me awake and we ate a little bit. Salma said she was going to go to the market again and when she came back the dishes must be washed and we must be sitting at the table quietly chatting. After about ten minutes since Salma left, I had told the boys everything I heard.

CHAPTER 6

"There's no way!"exclaimed Manka, slamming the kitchen table with his hand. "No way at all!"

"Listen, I heard her myself," I said.

"But if she does turn one of us into a wolf…" Deso trailed off. "What would we do?"

"I told you. She said something about going to the very end of the kingdom near a pond that is so shiny it makes the most golden coin look dull, and looking for a woman that calls herself Mama Menny," I said.

"Well then, let's run away now!" said Manka.

"We can't. That woman she was with—Jain—asked the same thing. What if we run away? The old woman, her name is Salma by the way, said that she memorized our scent and she'd find us."

"So what do we do? I hear witches never die."

"Well, according to Salma, she said that she can die if she's set on fire or someone sticks a branch from one of these trees outside into her left eye." The boys stared at me.

"Yeah, I know it's weird but that's what she said."

"So let's set her on fire!" said Deso. "It would do the world a favor."

"We can't just set her on fire; we need a plan of some sort. If we don't do it correctly she might still live and kill us all," I pointed out.

"I have an idea!" exclaimed Deso, jumping up from the table. "Have you heard of the story of Hansel and Gretel?" he asked. Manka and I both nodded. "Why don't we do the same thing? Push her into the fireplace!"

"That…is actually not a bad idea!" I said. "Good thinking, Deso! But we need to make sure it turns out perfectly. I'll do the same thing as Gretel. If she asks me how to do something over the fireplace, I'll push her in."

"Make sure the fire is well fed though," advised Manka.

"Of course," I said.

We had our plan and we were going to get out of this hell house alive!

We quickly washed dishes, and as Salma told us to be, we were sitting at the table, chatting quietly about things like puppies and cats and what it would be like to own one.

"Good! Everything is clean!" Salma said as she walked through the door. For about two weeks, everything went along fine. As soon as Salma left we started cleaning and talking about how we were going to push her into the fire. But one day, Salma crossed the line.

"Children, come here!" called Salma. We were in the back room talking quietly. We came over to her.

"I have something to say," said Salma, sitting up straight as she could with her hunched back. "I am going to change each and every one of your names into something nicer."

"Why?" I blurted out. "I like my name."

Salma stared at me for a minute before answering, "Flame does not suit a pretty girl such as yourself. It is too harsh too…wild."

"So what kind of name will I have?" I asked.

"I think Rose will be perfect."

"Rose?" said Deso, disgusted. "Personally, I don't like that name at all." I stepped on Deso's foot to keep him quiet.

"Personally, I don't care," said Salma. "Now, you two, brown head, your name will be Michael, and you, blondie, yours shall be…James. Also, I would like for you all to call me a new name…" she paused dramatically, "Mother."

"I can't," I said firmly.

"And why not?" asked Salma, her voice heated with anger.

"My mother is dead and I don't think—"

"Well then you should have no problem calling me Mother then, right? Considering yours is dead and here I am!" Salma's sneer was terrible.

Not for long, I thought. I struggled to say the one word. "Yes."

"Yes what?" Salma was enjoying this.

"Yes…Mother."

Salma showed her toothless smile again. "Good. And I want you two to also call me Mother."

"Yes, Mother," Deso, now James, and Manka, now Michael, both said at the same time.

After a couple more minutes of Salma enjoying our new names and enjoying how we called her Mother, she left to go visit a friend.

"I shall be back in one hour. You shall be sleeping by the time I come back. Good-bye, Michael, James, and Rose!" Salma said.

I flinched at my name but said with Deso and Manka, "Good-bye, Mother!"

We waited until she was gone and then I blurted out, "She has to go. How could she change my name? Rose... unbelievable."

"I know!" cried Deso. "And me...James? Do I look like a James to you?" I shook my head.

"And me, Michael!" said Manka. "I do not look like a Michael! Do I?" I shook my head again.

"So when are we going to do it?" asked Deso.

"I think tonight. I can't stand the fact that she wants us to call her mother!"

"Unbearable," Manka agreed.

After forty-five minutes of talking about how much we hated Salma, we went to bed. Salma came in twenty minutes later and opened the door quietly. Someone was whispering behind her. Deso and Manka were fast asleep, but I kept my ears open.

"Close the door quietly, Jain," said Salma. The door shut silently and they stopped in front of us.

"You know, I renamed them," Salma whispered.

"What did you name them?"

"Well, the girl is now Rose, the blonde is now James, and the brown-haired one is Michael."

"Those are all lovely names, especially for the girl. What did you say her name used to be?"

"Flame."

"Oh, what an ugly name!" exclaimed Jain.

"Yes, that is why I had to change it!" said Salma. "Well, come on, into the back room." They crossed over us and went into the back room. For a while they talked about Jain's families and other boring things. Then, finally, an interesting subject came up.

"So when are you going to turn the boy into a wolf?" asked Jain.

"Probably tonight. I think I will say something to make him mad, so that will give me an excuse," said Salma.

"But why are you just doing it? Has he even said anything out of line since the last time?" asked Jain.

"No, he has not. But it has been a while since I have turned somebody into an animal and I don't want to forget how. Anyway, the boy has given me so much trouble! I honestly think I'll turn him into a wolf tonight and then we can eat him for dinner. I shall make the girl make a nice hot fire and she can cook him in the pot."

That will be my chance to kill you, I thought.

"Oh, Salma, your mind is as brilliant as always!" said Jain.

"Yes, well…it comes with experience."

Again, they kept talking about boring subjects until Jain said, "I would love to talk to them."

"Of course, anything for you, Jain!" exclaimed Salma. She walked over to us and shook us awake. We all sat up abruptly.

"What's going on?" Manka sounded very confused and his words all tied in together.

"Get up," Salma commanded. "I want you to meet my good friend, Jain."

We all sat up and I finally got to see Jain. She had shoulder-length, dirty-blonde hair with a smile so wide I thought she could have eaten us all with one bite. She was very thin, lean, and so tall that she almost reached the ceiling of the cottage. She had jangling bracelets on both hands, and on her left hand was a big bag that looked like it was bursting at the seams.

She smiled, if possible, even wider at us. "Hello, children!" she said.

We mumbled "Hi" back.

She toted her tongue. "Now, now, children, I couldn't exactly hear you. What did you say to your Aunt Jain?"

Aunt Jain? God, they're all out of their minds, I thought.

"Hi!" said Manka so loudly he was almost yelling.

Jain turned to Salma and whispered, "I can see what you mean."

Salma just nodded and said, "This is Rose." She pointed at me.

"This is James." She pointed at Deso.

"And this is Michael." She pointed at Manka who started waving furiously at Jain. "Children, this is my good friend, Jain. You will now call her Aunt Jain, just as you have called me Mother. Understand?"

"Yes, Mother," we said simultaneously. We had some lunch and then we all had to walk Jain back to her house. The trip was slow and boring, and I was so scared that Salma was going to turn Manka into a wolf at any second. The worst part was that we couldn't even talk. We had to trail behind Salma and Jain and listen to their boring conversation about some man named Phillip who was cheating on his wife Macy, who was actually seeing another man Tim, who was seeing Macy's best friend Kathryn, who was actually in love with Macy's husband Phillip!

I had memorized the way to get to Jain's house. By the time we finally got there, it was about an hour till sundown. We said good-bye to Jain and left to go back to our cottage. I knew what was waiting back at the cottage. I did not want Manka to be turned into a wolf. As soon as we got back home, Salma made a spill.

"Clean it up!" she snapped at me. I grabbed a rag, but Manka stopped me.

"I'll do it," he said.

"Manka stop. Remember what I told you?" I whispered. But Manka paid no attention. He started to clean it up instead of me. Salma was furious.

"Put the rag down, boy! Let Rose clean it up!"

"No," Manka said firmly and he continued to wipe up the spill.

"What did you say?"

"Mother!" I called, breaking up the argument. "Mother, I want to make some tea, but I can't seem to do it! Can you help me?"

"Of course, dear." Salma walked over to me. "Feed the fire more. Make it bigger," she commanded.

I put so much wood in the fireplace it almost didn't fit. The fire was blazing now and it was so hot I could feel it from the back room.

"Open some windows so the smoke doesn't get stuck inside this house," commanded Salma.

"Yes, Mother," I replied. I opened the window and the door so we could make a quick escape afterward. Salma put water in a kettle and showed me where to put it. I put it high above the fire so I could push in Salma later. Manka and Deso were relaxing by the table. I took the kettle off the fire. I would get to push Salma into the fire any second now...

"What are you two doing just relaxing?" Salma scolded.

"Well, we've been working hard all day and then we had to walk your little friend home with you, which took incredibly long considering you don't know how to walk!" replied Manka.

"What did I say about talking back, Michael?" sneered Salma.

"*My name is not Michael!*"

"How dare you speak to your mother like that?" burst Salma.

"You are not my mother!"

Salma stood in place for a moment shaking with anger.

"Fine," she said at last. "Well, Michael, I warned you not to cross me. You did not listen. Now, I must do something that I do not want to."

"Then don't do it." Deso came out from nowhere.

"Very well," said Salma, glaring at Deso, "I will deal with you after I deal with Michael."

I knew what was coming. She started mumbling under her breath. She raised her hands above her head.

"NO!" I yelled.

But it was too late. A blinding flash went through the house like a bolt of lightning and it blasted me backwards into the wall. I opened my eyes and there, instead of Manka, stood a beautiful brown wolf.

CHAPTER 7

"How could you?" I yelled. I was furious.

"I did what I had to do," said Salma. "And now it's your turn." She pointed at Deso. She started mumbling.

"Oh, no, you don't!" I lunged at her and knocked her to the ground.

"*Rose!* What do you think you're doing?" Salma said.

"Number one," I said—my hands were clenched in fists and I was ready to fight—"my name is not Rose, it's Flame. Number two, you are not going to touch Deso, you little witch!"

Salma got up. She walked in front of the fire, which was burning high now. I saw my chance. I ran at her and pushed her in.

"*Nooo! What are you doing to me? Aaahhhh!*" screamed Salma. She was on fire now, but she still got out and came for me. I tried to dodge her, but she grabbed hold of my wrist.

"*If I am going to die you are going to die with me, you little brat!*" she yelled.

"Let me go!" I screamed. Her grip was too strong. Salma started walking toward the fire with me. I was so close to being burnt alive right then and there. I was not ready to die. All I did my whole life was steal. And now that was how it was going to end.

Deso came to the rescue yet again. He grabbed her arm and made her let go of me. Then, he pushed her into the fire once more.

"*Aaaahhhh! Noooo!*" screamed Salma. "*How could you, after all I've done for you! Ahhh...*" Her screams slowly died away. I stood on the spot shaking. My whole life could have ended with the witch dragging me away to my death.

"You okay?" asked Deso. He came over to me. I wrapped my arms around myself and shook my head. I was close to tears. Deso embraced me in a hug.

"Thank you," I whispered.

I grabbed a pitcher of water and put out the fire. There was nothing there. No bones, no skeleton, nothing. Nothing but a little bracelet was lying in the grey ashes. I bent over to pick it up, but a hand grabbed me around my waist and pulled me back up.

"What do you think you're doing?" asked Deso. His eyes were furious.

"Picking up her bracelet. We might need it," I replied.

"What if it does something to you?" asked Deso. "What if you become like her?"

"All right, fine," I said. I went to the kitchen, got a few rags and some string, and I picked up the bracelet with the rag, put it in some more rags, and tied it all together with the string. I took the satchel and put the bracelet inside. "Happy?" I asked.

"Not really," replied Deso. A low whine came from under the table. I had completely forgotten that Manka was a wolf now!

"Oh, my gosh, Manka! Are you okay?" I asked. Deso knelt beside me.

"What did you say Salma said about some lady?" asked Deso.

"Um...she said something about a woman, Mama Menny, who could bring people who have been turned into animals back into their human form."

"And where does she live?"

"Far away from the castle, near a pond that is so shiny it makes the most golden coin seem dull."

"Well then, come on! Let's go see this Mama Menny!" said Deso.

"How about tomorrow?" I asked. "We need to rest right now."

"I honestly don't think that I could spend another day in this house." I looked at him, begging with my eyes.

"All right, I guess one more day couldn't hurt," agreed Deso. The next day, as soon as we were up, we packed up. We grabbed a different satchel that Salma had and packed it with food and jars and canteens with water.

"Oh, yeah, Manka, by the way, you can turn into a human for an hour every day if you concentrate long enough. And if you need to turn back into a wolf you have to concentrate really hard," I said. A low whine came from Manka, saying he understood.

"I think we'll have to get food by day and travel at night," said Deso. "If people see us with a wolf they will freak out."

"Good idea," I agreed. "If we're out buying food and water, Manka will stay in the forest and we'll come back to him when we're done." Then a thought accorded to me, "What if we travel at the edge of the woods?"

"And meet more freaks like Salma?" asked Deso. "No, thank you! Maybe Manka can stay in the woods during the nights and we can stay in a house. Then in the morning we will bring breakfast and things like that to him."

"But then when will we travel?" I asked.

"Good point…Okay, how about this, we can travel during the day at the edge of the forest. Then at night, we will go to an inn or a house and Manka can sleep in the woods, and in the morning we will bring breakfast to him and keep on traveling."

"I'm fine with that," I said. "What about you, Manka?"

Manka pawed at the ground. I think he just didn't like the thought of being alone in the woods at night. We headed off. We got to the edge of the forest and started walking alongside it. We were making good progress. Before long, we were out of the woods and near the kingdom.

"Do you think we should visit Jain?" I asked.

"Probably not," replied Deso. "She might go ballistic if she finds out we killed Salma and report us to the guards or something, and we don't need anymore trouble with them."

"You're right about Jain, but the guards have never even seen our faces, have they?" I asked.

"No, they haven't, but still, if Jain reports us we might go to jail because we set somebody on fire, and if we tell them that she was a witch they might kill us."

"Good point." We kept on walking, stopping for brief amounts of time to eat. After about two days of always being in the woods (we decided that we would just sleep in the woods with Manka, and one of us would keep watch at all times) a new problem occurred.

"We need food," Deso said one day, looking into the empty satchel.

"We don't have any money," I said.

Deso looked into the second satchel and pulled out a few items that I noticed were from Oliver's store.

"You don't think that I would've given it all to Virp, right?" asked Deso with a mischievous grin on his face. I could have jumped for joy.

"Okay, I'll go into town and get us some more food after I sell this stuff," I said.

"I'll come too," said Deso.

"Someone needs to stay here with Manka and it's not going to be me, you know I don't do well in the woods."

"You'll be with a wolf!" Deso pointed out.

"Well, yes, but…please just let me go into town by myself! I need to breathe some fresh air. Next time you'll go. I promise."

Deso seemed somewhat against the idea, but he let me go by myself. Sunlight hit my face as soon as I walked out and I smiled. It was so good to be back. I was in the town's center and it smelled so good. Bread coming out of the bakery was so fresh you could smell it from a mile, the candy shop was bursting with sweets, and the entertainers were walking down the streets playing their beautiful music, sticking out their hats so someone could chip in a gold coin. I started walking to a store where I could sell the item Deso gave to me. But after a couple of minutes, I noticed that someone was following me. I turned around.

"Deso," I said. "I thought we agreed you would stay with Manka!"

He shrugged. "He told me to go," he replied. "He turned back into a human for a second and said 'go get some fresh air, I'll be fine,' so I went. And I told him we would be back before sundown."

I shook my head in disbelief. "I'll never be by myself if I'm with one of you, will I?" I asked.

"Oh, come on, Flame," said Deso. "Well, if we're going to be back by sundown, we ought to start walking to sell this thing." The thing, of course, was the object from Oliver's store, and it was a little statue of a man praying to one of the gods. We sold the little statue to a man who happily gave us ten dollars for it, and we set off to buy the food. We got to the center of town. I never realized how beautiful it was because I was always looking out for the guards. In the center, there was a gorgeous fountain made out of the finest white stone. The water spurting out of it was shooting high into the air. The stone for the street was so gorgeous it looked like it was placed there by angels, and it was shaped in big circles. The musicians came around to the center. Three men were playing instruments, one with the fiddle, another with a lyre, and the last one with a flute.

"Come on," I said to Deso.

"What?"

"Let's dance!" I said.

He shook his head. "I can't dance."

"Neither can I! Just…come on!" I took his hand and dragged him out to dance. Within seconds, people were joining us, dancing in circles in the town's center. After about ten minutes of dancing, Deso and I sat down by the fountain, breathing heavily. I walked over to the musicians and dropped three coins in the hat, walked back over to

Deso, and sat back down. After a few minutes of watching everybody else dance, a boy came up to me. He was tall, with light brown hair, and anyone could see he had muscles under his shirt. His eyes were the most blue I had ever seen, like two drops of the dark blue ocean got carried away by the wind and were caught in his lashes. He extended his arm to me.

"Would you like to dance?" he asked. His voice was smooth, as if every word he had said glided on ice before it had reached my ears. I was so breathless I could hardly say yes, all I did was nod. I thought I heard something like a grunt of jealousy from Deso behind me, but I didn't pay attention. I let the strange boy dance with me and spin me around so many times. I was so dizzy I thought I might have fallen, but the boy was always there to catch me.

After about three songs, the boy took my hand and kissed it lightly.

"I'm sorry, but I have to go now," he said, and he let go of my hand reluctantly.

"Wait! I don't even know your name!" I called after him, but he was already gone. I sat back down next to Deso.

"How was it?" he asked. What was it in his voice? Jealousy? Maybe mixed with a little bit of anger?

"It was fine," I said casually, not wanting to upset him more. We left to buy the food shortly after. We visited the dough-man and bought some bread, went to the well, drank our fill, and then filled up the canteens with water, and finally, we visited the butcher to get some meat for Manka who was starting to crave it more now that he was a wolf. The walk back was not long, and we reached Manka within minutes. He was sitting down where we left him, patiently waiting for us. He turned into a human, which looked weird. His nose seemed to grow back into his skull, his hair was shortened and looked as if it was also shooting back into his head, his legs began to lengthen and stand up on his hind legs, and his arms also lengthened a little. He stood up, and there was the familiar face of Manka I knew.

CHAPTER 8

Manka smiled widely at me. "How was it?" he asked.

"What? The town?" I asked. "It was nice."

"You brought meat, right?" he asked.

I chuckled. "Yes, Manka, I did." I took some meat wrapped up in paper and gave it to Manka. He turned back into a wolf so he could eat it. After we all ate, we started to travel some more.

After three more days and nights of being in the forest, we were almost at the end, where Mama Menny was supposed to live. On the fourth day, I spotted an incredibly shiny lake.

"Guys, I think I found it!" I exclaimed. And sure enough, near the lake was a little house. All of our energy rushed into us and we ran as fast as we could to the house. I knocked on the door and it almost immediately opened. An old black woman stood at the front door, dressed in a long dress that was decorated with flowers—it reached her feet. Her neck was showered in necklaces and from her ears were two, long, dangly, silver earrings.

"Mama Menny?" I asked.

"Yes, my child, that is me," she replied. "Come on in. I know you and your friends have been traveling for many, many days. Come, have a rest."

We all walked in, including Manka. Inside her house, there were about three or four rooms. As soon as you walked into the house, you could see a table and a fireplace. The walls were decorated with murals and strange symbols on the walls. Deso and I sat down at the table and Manka sat down next to us on the floor.

"I think I know what the problem is," said Mama Menny as she looked at Manka.

"Yes. We need help," I said.

"You want to make him human again, yes?" asked Mama Menny.

"Yes," I agreed.

"Then first I must ask you one question. Then I will tell you how to make him human again. How did he become to be a wolf in the first place?"

I told her our story. She sat there the whole time listening with her eyes closed and her head rocking back and forth slightly as if my words were like music to her. Finally, she opened her big brown eyes.

"You killed that witch, Salma?" she asked.

I nodded, scared that she liked Salma and wouldn't help us if she found out we killed her.

"Finally!" she exclaimed. "I have waited too long for her to die."

"You don't like her?" asked Deso.

"I despise her," she spat. "Making people work for her! You're lucky she liked you, little girl, otherwise you would have all been eaten that night!"

"She did say something about eating Manka after he had been turned into a wolf," I remembered.

"Aye. She would have eaten, first the wolf, then the other boy, and she would have kept you as her slave. You are very lucky that you heard what you did."

"So, she had done this before? What happened with the people?"

"Died or committed suicide. Could you imagine working for that woman for eternity?" she shuddered. "You did everyone good, children, believe me."

"So, now that we helped everyone, hopefully you can help us?" I asked.

Mama Menny smiled widely. "Of course, child," she said. "Listen carefully to what I am about to tell you. What you have heard from Salma is no lie. I can help your friend turn back into a human, but to do that, you must retrieve three pieces of an important stone. The three stone pieces are scattered across the land—and not just in our kingdom, in another one across the desert.

"The first one you must collect is in the heart of the desert itself. In the middle of the desert, there is an oasis, and in this oasis lies the first piece to the stone that you must receive. The second piece of the stone is where the mountains stand. In the mountains, you will find a crack in one of the boulders that are in the very front. You must search very carefully, for it is cleverly concealed. You must go through the crack, and there will be a path. You must follow the path the whole way. It will lead to a river. Never step off the path.

"To get the stone piece, you must talk to the merpeople that live there and get them to get the stone for you, because it is within their possession. And the third stone piece is at my cousin's house in the other kingdom—the Erkon Kingdom. He lives almost where I do, a little farther off than where the Erkon Castle is. If you tell him that I sent you, he will give you the stone piece. If you put these pieces together correctly, magic will send you back to the foot of my door. On the back of these pieces is a spell that only I can read. So you must bring back the stone to me. I will read the spell and your friend will turn back into a human. Do you understand, my children?" I nodded.

"You can set off tomorrow. But you sleep here tonight," said Mama Menny. I looked outside and saw that it had already grown dark. Mama Menny showed us where we could sleep, and we fell asleep right away. My last thought before I fell asleep was wondering if we would be able to collect all the pieces of the stone for Manka.

CHAPTER 9

I woke up to the sound of Mama Menny soothing someone with her calm voice.

"…don't have to worry anymore, child, they cannot get you in here. Sit, have something to eat." I heard a chair scrap against the wood floor as someone dragged it out. I sat up. A boy was sitting in a chair, his back to me so I couldn't see his face, but his light brown hair reminded me of someone, I just couldn't figure out who.

"Ah, good you are up," said Mama Menny. "Come, have breakfast while the others are still sleeping." I walked over to the table and sat down in a chair. I looked into the face of the boy and instantly I remembered who he was. His dark, sea-blue eyes looked into mine. He was the boy I danced with in the town's square.

"Remember me?" he asked. How smooth his voice was.

"Couldn't forget if I wanted to," I replied. He smiled and his brilliant white teeth shone.

"I never did get to find out your real name," I said.

He hesitated for a moment before telling me. "It's Eric."

"Flame."

Manka and Deso woke up and Deso joined us at the table, and Manka, in his wolf form, sat down next to me and nudged my hand onto the top of his head. Deso glared at the boy. He obviously remembered him as vividly as I did.

"So Mama Menny said you guys were going to the Erkon Kingdom," said Eric.

"Yeah, we're stopping by. Why?" asked Deso coldly.

"I need to hide out there for a while. I was wondering if I could tag-along."

"Sure, why not," I said. Deso threw a look at me.

"You ought to set off soon," said Mama Menny. "Right after you eat breakfast."

We had a nice breakfast of eggs and bread. Then we packed the satchel with bread and water, and before we set off, Mama Menny gave me a quilt.

"I always have it in case of an emergency. Trust me, you might need it." She smiled at me.

I took the quilt from her hands, it was soft but heavy, and I couldn't exactly see the design because it was folded, but it had a lot of dark blue on it.

"Thank you very much, Mama Menny," I said. She smiled again and stroked my hair. "Anytime, child. Now, be safe." We stepped out of the doorway and started walking toward the desert, which didn't seem too far away. We walked for about half an hour before reaching the sand of the desert.

"You guys ready?" I asked. I looked out into the desert. I could hardly see the mountains that lay behind it.

Manka made a small nod with his furry head.

"Ready," said Deso. Eric stayed silent.

We took our first step into the desert. We walked on for a while before I realized how hot it was getting. It was almost unbearable. I tied my hair up with a piece of cloth. We kept walking through the hot desert. After about an hour, I noticed we were slowing down.

"Flame...give me some water," begged Deso.

I passed a canteen over to him. "Don't drink too much," I told him. "We don't know how long we're going to be here." We suffered for the rest of the day, and when night finally came, we were all so exhausted that we just fell down in the sand and fell asleep. Suddenly, a voice was calling my name. I opened my eyes, looked up, and was frightened by what I saw. Salma's face was staring at me.

"Wake up, Rose," she said. "You're coming with me." She took my arm and dragged me upward.

"I'm not going!" I yelled. "Manka! Deso! *Help*!"

"It's no use," said Salma, dragging me across the desert, back the way I came. "They're already gone."

"What do you mean they're gone?" I asked.

"Don't you see, Rose? I only wanted you. The others were useless. The vultures will find them soon."

"*What?*" I yelled. Fear filled me. I looked back. The sun was rising and I could already see them. Manka was human again, sleeping, and so was Deso. But there was a pool of red around both of them, too red to be the sand. They weren't sleeping. I tackled Salma out of rage and started hitting her everywhere I could. I pinned her to the ground, my legs on her thighs and my arms around her wrists.

"*Bring them back*!" I yelled, tears streaming down my cheeks.

She laughed. "Stupid child," she said, "don't you know no one can bring back the dead?"

"*No! You have to!*" I screamed. She kept laughing. I noticed that even though the sun was rising, she was growing darker, like ash. I started to lose my grip on her. Next thing I knew, she was a dark vapor, and she shot toward my face. It was dark all around me. Her laugh was still echoing all around me. I sat up abruptly, breathing heavily. It was only a dream. I looked to my side, and Manka and Deso were still sleeping, and with no pool of blood around them. I looked around for a figure in the dark. There was nothing there. I took a shaky sigh of relief. I noticed something wet on my cheeks. I brushed my hand under my eye. Tears. I had actually cried. Something I swore off when Mom and Dad died. It was cool now that it was night. It would be a better time to travel. I went over to the boys and shook them awake.

"Wake up," I said. "It's better to travel at night." They all sat up groggily. The three of them had a piece of bread and some water. I didn't eat anything. After my dream, I was just glad to see Manka and Deso stand up. The moon was high above us as we walked, our shadows exaggerating how small I felt in the large desert. We all kept quiet, as we were all too tired to sleep.

"How much longer?" moaned Deso.

"I don't know," I replied. My throat was dry. I took a swig of water.

"What's our new plan?" asked Manka. He had turned back into a human for a little bit. "It's too hot to walk in the day and we're too tired to walk at night."

"I think we should walk during the day, and as night comes around you guys can fall asleep and I'll keep watch. We can sleep for a couple of hours and then we keep walking."

"And when are you going to sleep?" asked Eric.

"I don't know. Maybe we can switch off." We kept silent after that. We kept walking until the sun started to rise again and it started getting hot. We plopped down on the sand and ate some bread and drank some water, carefully saving it all. We kept walking. The sun beat down on us, and before long I thought I was starting to see hallucinations.

"Do you guys see a tree?" I asked. The boys squinted into the distance.

"No," they said. Manka shook his head.

"Splash some water on your face, Flame, I think you're hallucinating," said Deso. I took some water and splashed a little bit on my face, which helped for a while. We stopped again in the middle of the day to eat some bread and drink water.

"Funny how Mama Menny didn't say how long it would take to get to the oasis," said Deso.

"I don't think she knows either," I said between mouthfuls of bread. "Otherwise she would have told us."

After we finished breakfast, we all stood up against our wills and kept walking toward the mountains. Darkness fell too slowly. I could feel my face hurting. I must've been sunburned.

I didn't know how much longer I could hold up. The sun finally sank down into the earth, and the moon popped up. As soon as it started getting dark, the boys went to sleep and I stayed up and kept watch. Manka turned back into a human.

"Hey, Flame," he said, "When the moon gets a little higher, wake me up and I'll keep watch, okay?"

I nodded. He lay down on the ground, back in his wolf form, and fell asleep almost instantly. I sat in the sand, making sure nothing was coming. I was especially watching out for a small figure moving across the sand. I kept Manka's promise and woke him when the moon was a little higher in the sky. I lay down in the sand and Manka kept watch as a wolf. He only had about an hour or two of sleep, but he said he was fine. I fell asleep before my head hit the sand. I was sitting in a kitchen. Salma's kitchen.

"Dinner!" said Salma, and she put a bowl in front of me. The soup was a dark red, and there were vegetables floating around in it.

"What's in it?" I asked.

I looked around the room and found Deso's shirt on the chair next to me.

"I told you your friends were useless," she replied. I looked in the cauldron where the rest of the soup was and I saw something that looked like an ear. A wolf's ear. I screamed as loud as I could, and before I knew it, Deso was next to me, soothing my hair. I buried my face in his shirt and he hugged me back.

"Where's Manka?" I whispered.

"I'm right here," he said. He was sitting right next to me. I let go of Deso and hugged Manka as hard as I could. I wasn't about to sleep anymore.

"Flame, what happened?" Manka asked, soothing my hair like Deso did.

"Nightmare," I whispered.

"What happened in it?"

I told them about my nightmare. It was a short one, so it didn't take too long to explain. Manka and Deso paid very close attention, and Eric stayed quiet, looking at the ground. He looked like he was too scared to even look at me.

"Well, the important thing is that she's dead," said Manka. "Trust me, she's dead." I nodded.

"Let's start walking," I said. The boys nodded and stood up. We walked through the night, always going forward. I kept looking around to make sure Salma wasn't following us. Deso must've noticed because he put a hand on my shoulder and said, "Don't worry. I promise you, she's dead." Soon, the sun started to rise and I felt as if my body was on fire from the heat.. I thought I saw a tree, but I was also probably hallucinating. I decided to ask anyways.

"Do you guys see a tree?" I asked.

Deso squinted. "Actually, yes, I do," he replied.

"Me too," said Eric.

Manka pawed the ground.

"If there's a tree there, it needs water. And where there's water in the middle of the desert…" We all stopped and looked at each other for a brief moment, and then we all broke into a run toward the tree. We sprinted for five minutes before we finally reached the tree, and sure enough, there was a whole pool of water. We sank to our knees and started to drink the water with our cupped hands. Except for Manka, who just lapped up the water with his tongue. I filled up all of the canteens again and put them back into the satchel. I looked in the middle of the oasis. There, in the water, standing on what looked like a pillar, was a rock. It was cracked on one side, as if someone had broken it. We had found the first stone piece.

"Guys, there it is!" I said. "I'll go get it." I took off my shoes and stepped into the water. It felt so good between my hot and tired toes. That's when everything went wrong. The water started bubbling.

CHAPTER 10

Deso pulled me back out of the water, but it still kept bubbling.

"I didn't do it!" I said. It was one of the things I learned to say when I was living with the nuns. I was always causing trouble, but almost never got caught. Deso looked at me. I shrugged. The whole oasis was bubbling now. And I could see something rising out of the water. Its head came out of the water fast, and in ten seconds I could see what it was. A dragon. It was ruby red with glowing green eyes. It actually looked quite beautiful. But that moment passed once it started to breathe fire at us. We all ducked out of the way and the fire melted some of the sand. I took out my pocket knife. But what good would that do against a huge fire-breathing monster?

"How are we going to kill it?" asked Deso.

"I don't know!" I yelled back. "Try to find a weak spot!"

"*How?*"

"See if it's hiding something! Something it doesn't want us to attack! *Duck!*" Just then, the dragon took a deep breath and started to breathe even more fire. While it was distracted with trying to kill us, I ran around the back of it and tried to see if there was something that I could attack, something that could kill it. Then, I noticed something; its wings were folded awkwardly. As its wings expanded, I could see something shiny on his back.

That might be his weak spot, I thought. I quickly ran back over to Deso.

"You guys distract it, I'm going to go kill it!" I said.

"What?" yelled Deso, but I had already left. I was behind the dragon and its tail was on the sand. I went over and carefully jumped on one of the spikes on its back so it wouldn't feel me on him. I kept climbing on the spikes on his back until I got to where his wings were. He took another deep breath in, and that's when I slipped. His body gave an unexpected shudder and my foot slipped and touched his back. The dragon started to flip out and he started to fling his body sideways. I held on tightly, but my hands were slipping. I was so close to the weak spot. Next thing I knew, the dragon started to flap its wings. It lifted up into the air.

"*Flame!*" Deso cried.

I held on for dear life as the dragon started flipping upside down. Don't ask me how I did it because I have no idea either. All I know is one minute he's leaving the oasis and then he started to circle back. He was still upside down, trying to get me off, sometimes making sharp turns, and I was about to fall. The spikes on his back were slippery. I got a tighter grip on his spikes and got my foot off of his back. He turned right side-up and I was careful not to make any noises. He landed back into the oasis and took another deep breath. I took this chance to dig my pocketknife into the little spot in his back. Stabbing the dragon was like cutting through a cake right out of the oven—it felt very soft compared to its rough scales on his body. A pool of warm blood from the dragon flowed onto my hand, making the dragon rear back unexpectedly and I fell off and into the water. Good thing I knew how to swim. I swam to the shore and the dragon was still swarming around, making awful screeching sounds. My pocketknife stayed in his back when I fell off. He thrashed for half a minute before he finally fell dead on the shore..

I saw Manka turn back into a human as I ran towards him, Deso, and Eric. "Oh, god, Flame!" Manka exclaimed when he saw me. He grabbed me by the shoulders. "Are you out of your mind?!" he scolded.

I looked at him. "Yes." I said simply. He stood there, stunned. I broke out laughing. Manka looked mad at me.

"Aw come on, Manka, no harm no foul. I'm fine and we're about to go get a stone piece for you to turn you back into a human soon." There was a huge explosion behind Manka,. The dragon had exploded, along with my pocketknife. The pocketknife that my dad gave me before he died. After the smoke had cleared, a white figure rose from the ashes. It was a woman.

"Thank you for freeing me," she said. Her voice was gentle and soft. She looked quite young—a woman in her twenties. Her curly hair went down past her shoulders and her eyes had a sort of blaze in them.

"Since you freed me I must repay you. I can give you anything you like."

"Are you a ghost?" asked Manka.

"No. No, I am simply a spirit who was sacrificed to that dragon who now lies in ashes. For hundreds of years I have been trying to get out of his stomach, but never could until now. You four freed me, and I thank you for that. Now, what shall you like in return?"

"I kind of want my pocketknife back," I said.

"You mean this one?" The spirit lifted her hand and my knife came out of the ashes. The same old knife. I ran toward it and grabbed it.

"Thanks!" I said.

"Is there any way you could get us to those mountains?" asked Deso.

Her face grew grave. "I am not allowed to leave this oasis for this is where I died. But I can make the journey a lot easier."

"How?"

"I can make sure you always have an unlimited supply of food and water and money and I can make the sun beat down less on you."

"Please?" pleaded Deso. The woman waved her hand.

"Granted," she said. I instantly felt a cool wind sweep over me and felt the satchel on my shoulder get heavier.

"Is there any way you can make me stay as a human longer?" asked Manka.

The woman stared at him. "What do you mean by that?" she asked.

Manka turned into a wolf, demonstrating what he meant. He turned back into a human.

"I've been cursed," he said. "I can only turn human for an hour a day. Is there any way you can…extend that period of time?"

"I am sorry, but I cannot," said the woman. "A witch's power is beyond my own."

Manka looked down at the ground. "I understand," he said, sounding disappointed.

"I really am sorry," she said. "Anything else?"

"Yeah, can we have that stone please?" I asked.

"Which one?"

"The one in the middle of the oasis, on that pillar thing."

"Oh, yes of course." The stone disappeared from the pillar in the water and appeared in my hand. The gorgeous red rock reflected everything that shined on it. The side of the rock that had been broken was smoothly cut off by something.

"Thank you very much," I said.

"Is there anything else?"

We all shook our heads.

"Well then," said the woman, "safe journey to you all." She sank back into the water.

I put the rock in the satchel. One down, two to go.

CHAPTER 11

We all decided that a quick swim would ease everything. We took off the top layers of our clothes and went swimming. It wasn't exactly swimming, considering the water wasn't exactly deep enough, but we did sit in the water and cool off a little bit. We sat there until the sun didn't beat down so hard, and then we walked around to dry off and continued with our journey.

"You do realize that if it took us about two and a half days to get to the oasis, which is supposed to be in the middle of the desert, then it's going to take us another two and a half days just to get to the mountains, right?" asked Deso while we were walking.

"Yes, I realized that," I replied. "Maybe we can make it one and a half days if we walk fast enough and don't take as many breaks. I mean, that spirit lady did say that she would make the sun beat down on us less so that will help, won't it?"

We picked up our pace and started walking a little bit faster. By the time the sun had set, I could hardly see the oasis anymore.

Deso volunteered to have the first watch, so the rest of us could sleep. I told him to wake me up when he got tired, which I knew would be soon. Eric lay down a little bit farther than the rest of us did, and I fell asleep on Manka's paws.

Someone was shaking me.

"Hey, Flame, can you keep watch for a while?" Deso's voice. I lifted my head off of Manka's paws.

"Yea, 'course," I said. I yawned widely.

"Never mind, I can finish the watch, I'll be fine," said Deso.

"No, go to sleep. I'll be fine," I protested.

He didn't argue further. He put his hand under his arm and fell asleep. I stayed up watching the moon and trying to count the stars. When the moon was high over our heads, I woke everyone up and we kept walking. We walked further and further into the desert. The mountains never seemed to be getting closer anyways, but I found out that when I looked down for a while and then looked back up, they did seem closer than before. Because the spirit gave us unlimited food and water, we had more energy and could walk faster, so we got through the desert quicker. The sun rose and we all groaned, but the heat wasn't as bad as it was a couple of days ago. I guess the spirit really did have powers.

And everything was going fine. Until Eric decided to speak his mind.

"I'm tired," he groaned.

"Why should you be tired?" spat Deso. "You're getting a lot of food and water and you're never on watch!"

"I hardly get sleep!" yelled Eric.

"Compared to Flame, you get a lot of sleep! She's gotten less sleep than the rest of us and you don't see her complaining do you?"

"This isn't about Flame! I'm just saying that I'm tired because I didn't get sleep!"

I saw something blurry go past me and I heard grunts of pain. Deso and Eric were fighting.

"Guys stop!" I yelled. They ignored me and kept rolling on the ground, punching and kicking anything. Manka turned into a human and watched them fight. I ran to break up the fight.

"Don't," said Manka. "Let them fight it out."

"And let them beat each other half to death? No." I ran right into the fight and tried to pull them apart. I got tripped and I fell into the fight. I knew they weren't hitting me on purpose, but either way, I was getting punched and kicked everywhere. I finally got in the middle of them and extended my arms and pulled them off of each other.

"Stop fighting!" I yelled. They both stared at me, panting. My head, eyes, and body were throbbing from where they were hitting me.

"Oh, my god, Flame, did we hit you?" asked Deso.

"Yeah, a little," I replied bitterly.

"I'm sorry," said Eric.

"We shouldn't fight, especially not over something as stupid as who got more sleep than who. I don't care if I get less sleep than all of you, I'll be fine. So there's no need to fight about it because I'll live. It's a stupid thing to be fighting about right now. What we need to focus on this moment is finding the stone pieces for Manka, okay?" The boys nodded. I took a sigh of relief.

"Can we keep walking now?" I asked. They nodded again. Manka turned back into a wolf and we kept walking in silence. Later that day, we stopped for a lunch break, ate and drank our fill, and kept walking. When it started to grow dark, Eric volunteered for first watch.

"Wake me up when you get tired," Deso said. We all fell asleep. I was walking along the town's square in the Arona Kingdom. I was all alone, which was strange because usually the square was bustling with activity. A shadow moved a couple of feet in front of me.

"Hello?" I said. "Who's there?"

Nothing answered me back. I kept walking. It was broad daylight, I was sure to see something if it came near me. Something moved behind an alley again. I could see a glimpse of the shadow. I was hoping it would be a stray cat but it was in the shape of a human.

"Oh, dear!" cried a voice behind me. I quickly spun around and saw that an old woman had dropped a basket of fruits in it. I breathed a sigh of relief.

"Do you need help?" I asked.

"That would be lovely, dear," said the old woman. I came over to her, helped pick up the fruits, and put them back into the basket. The woman stood up again. She was old and had gray, stringy hair. Her penetrating saucer-like eyes were grey, her back was hunched, and her bony hands were curled.

"Thank you, my dear Rose," said the old woman.

I froze. "What did you call me?" I asked.

The woman's lips curved into a thin, mocking smile. "Don't you remember your own mother?" she said. She started to change her form, and in two seconds stood Salma, right in front of me. Why hadn't I realized before? I should've recognized her voice.

"Come on, we're going home, Rose," said Salma. "Your dinner's ready." An image of the blood red soup came into my mind. She took my hand before I could react and started dragging me toward the Dark Forest.

"*No you can't make me!*" I yelled. "*No, no, no, no, no!*"

"Flame, wake up!" I heard a voice say from far away.

"*No, I won't go back!*" I screamed.

"Flame, wake up!" the voice said again. I opened my eyes. The moon was high and the stars were twinkling above me. Deso was holding me in his arms. I realized I was in a cold sweat and breathing heavily. I sat up. The boys were in a circle around me.

"It was her again," I said. "I was walking in the town's square and this old woman dropped her basket. I helped her pick up all the things that were in it and she called me Rose and then transformed into Salma and started dragging me toward the Dark Forest saying dinner was ready and the dinner was you guys." I drew in a shaky breath and let it out.

"Flame, I'm going to make you a promise," said Deso. "I promise that as long as you are here with either me or Manka, nothing will hurt you, especially Salma, even though she's dead. Okay?" I nodded.

"Let's keep walking," suggested Manka. We all stood up and started walking. By the time the sun rose, it seemed like we were very close to the mountains. We kept walking the entire day, taking brief rests to eat and hardly talking. I kept thinking about that shape-shifter in my dream and how she turned into Salma. Even though it was a dream, it still scared me. We spent another day walking and feeling like we accomplished nothing. By the time the moon came out, we were all exhausted. The spirit may have given us unlimited food and water and made the sun beat down on us less, but we were still tired of walking so much, and all of our feet hurt.

"They seem so close, but why aren't they coming?" groaned Eric. I knew he meant the mountains. We kept walking in the desert and I could feel myself falling asleep.

"Hey, guys?" I said. "Maybe we should stop and sleep for a little bit."

"We'll all fall asleep and get eaten," replied Deso. I groaned. Everything started to swirl before my eyes. My vision went dark and I fell.

CHAPTER 12

I was rocking, as if I was on a ship. Someone was holding my arms together around their neck. I opened my eyes and saw gold hair in front of them. I smiled.

"I can walk now," I said. Deso jumped, not knowing I was awake, but kept carrying me.

"Deso, it's okay, I can walk now," I repeated.

"No, you can't. Last time you were walking you blacked out." He gave a little jump to put me higher on his waist.

"How long have you been carrying me?" I asked.

"Half an hour?" Deso guessed. "You've been out longer, but we've been switching off. We're almost there. I can carry you the rest of the way."

"But I can walk!" I argued.

Deso stopped walking and turned his face in my direction. "I'll carry you the rest of the way. We're almost there. Stop complaining." He kept walking. I stopped complaining and let Deso carry me. We started to get very close to the base of the mountains.

"Manka," Deso said, "your turn."

"You guys, I can walk!" I said.

Manka turned back into a human. "Well, who said we're going to let you?" he asked. He smiled widely. Manka got close to Deso and they transported me onto Manka's back.

"Manka, you only have a limited time of being a human. I don't want you to carry me!" I yelled.

"Since when does anyone care about what you want?" asked Manka airily. Of course he was joking, but it still made me mad. Still, if they wanted to suffer with my weight on their back, let them do it. Within twenty minutes we got to the base of the mountains. It was getting dark so that meant it would be harder to see the crack in the mountains.

"Wait, where's the quilt Mama Menny gave to us?" I asked.

"Eric's carrying it," replied Deso. I looked over and saw Eric carrying the quilt Mama Menny gave us. He looked very hot and very tired from carrying it.

"Here, let me." I slid off Manka's back, despite his protests, and walked over to Eric, stumbling a little bit the first couple of steps. I took the quilt out of his hands. We started to walk along the mountains, trying to see if there was a crack anywhere in the mountains. We all split up and after about twenty minutes of searching, Eric found it.

"Hey, you guys, I think I found it," he called over to us. We all rushed over there. He was standing in front of some bushes waiting for us. He pushed them aside and there was a small hole in it. I stuck my head in it and I was amazed to see a whole path before my eyes.

"I think he found it," I said. "Let's go." We all climbed in through the hole and started walking again. We stayed on the path, like Mama Menny told us to do.

"Let's stop for the night," Eric said.

"I second that statement," agreed Deso. We dropped everything and I kept the first watch. Manka was sleeping in wolf form and I gave Deso and Eric the quilt to keep warm. I laid down on my back and tried to count the stars again, finding it to be impossible. I woke them up a couple of hours later and we kept walking. We were walking on a dirt path with the mountains high on each side. Trees were surrounding us on both sides.

"Did she say how long we're supposed to be walking until we find these mer-people?" asked Eric.

"I don't think so," I said. All of a sudden the mountain went down into a deep slope. I could hear a river.

"Probably not much longer," I replied. We started to go down the slope and one by one we all slipped and rolled down. A bunch of sticks and rocks slammed into me. When we got to the bottom, we all stayed on the ground for a little bit, trying to get over the pain. Manka was the first one to get up. He turned into a human and extended his arm to me. I grabbed it and he pulled me up.

"You're bleeding," he told me.

"Where?" I asked.

He took a leaf from the ground, pressed it against my head for a second, took it off, and showed it to me. The leaf was stained with blood.

"Well, what do you know," I said. "I really am bleeding. I'll be fine. And you're bleeding too."

"What? No, I'm not," said Manka.

I rolled up his sleeve. A pool of blood surrounded his arm.

"Oh…that's nothing," Manka said, pulling down his sleeve. Deso got up and immediately doubled over in pain.

Manka ran over to him and put Deso's arm over his shoulder. He had gotten cut up really bad, and it was in the same place that the wolf had bitten him when we fought against them.

"Oh, that's not good," I said when I saw the blood.

"There's not that much blood," said Eric, who finally stood up, a couple of scratches up and down his body.

"I know, but it stings because I got bit by a wolf there," said Deso. Eric looked over at Manka.

"No, it wasn't him," said Deso. "It was an actual wolf."

"The river's got to be getting close," I said. "We can help Deso there and clean ourselves up."

I gave Eric the quilt and put Deso's other arm around my shoulder. Once we finally saw the blue glimmer of a river, we set Deso down on a big rock. I took the quilt from Eric and unfolded it. It was a very big quilt—the four of us could lie down underneath it comfortably and not even touch each other. In the middle of it was a picture of the woods. Three figures stood in the background, their faces not visible.

The first was a wolf, sitting on its hind legs. The second was the figure of a girl, one hand on the shoulder blades of the wolf, her other hand was intertwined with the third figure who was a boy. They were staring up at a full moon as if they were either waiting for something or just enjoying the scenery. The rest of the quilt was a night blue with little spots in it, being the stars. I smiled. Mama Menny probably made this quilt the night that we came into her house. I rolled up Deso's shirt to where he got cut. There was a deep gash made into his side, probably by a stick, and it was still bleeding quite fast. Deso was starting to lose his color.

"Roll him over to his side," I said. Manka put him on the ground and put him on his side. I went over to the river, cupped my hands together, scooped up some water, and poured it on Deso's side. He took in a sharp breath.

"Sorry," I said, "but it should help stop the bleeding a little bit."

"How do you know?" asked Deso.

"What, you don't trust me?" I asked. I poured water on his side a couple more times and it stopped bleeding so bad. I took out my knife and went to the quilt. I cut a strip of the quilt off at the very bottom. Because the strip was so long, I also cut the strip in half, down by the middle. I took one half and dipped it in the river. I went over to Deso and wrapped it around him. Then, I took the dry piece and wrapped it around him, tying it tight at the end.

"Thanks," said Deso.

I folded the blanket, gave it to Eric, put Deso's arm over my shoulder with Manka, and we kept walking up the river. I couldn't even tell for how long we kept walking. All I know is that after an incredibly long time of walking, we finally came to the mouth of the river.

We sat down and rested. I looked into the water and saw something quickly swim by. I stood up and walked over to the edge of the water and looked in it. It was very clear and very deep. It got darker at the bottom. Something swished past me again, and it was bigger than a fish. My curiosity got to the best of me. I leaned in even further and closer, my nose was almost touching the water.

Something started to come up from the bottom of the river very slowly. It had a human-shaped head, and the color of its skin was a watery gray. It had eyes of perfect circles and they were an incredible light green. The mouth was also very human-like, and it was almost smiling at me as it was swimming up.

I smiled back at it as it swam up. All of a sudden, it rushed toward me, jumped out of the water, grabbed my hand, and dragged me into the water. I hardly took in a breath before it dragged me in. I tried fighting against it, but it was no use. It was stronger than me and it was dragging me toward the bottom. I was running out of breath and the pressure of the water was crushing me.

All of a sudden, I felt something tug at my other arm, trying to pull me upward, back to the surface. Both of the creatures started fighting over me. But it didn't matter anymore because I was about to suffocate. I had no more strength to even open my eyes. I had no more air left in my lungs. I blacked out, once again. I was sitting behind a table, and my mother was there sitting next to me. I was only about six or seven-years-old. The image of my mom was very faded, but I still knew it was her.

"Mommy, where's Daddy?" I asked. She was staring blankly into the air. "Mommy?" I said. She looked at me. "Where's Daddy?" I repeated. She swallowed and I could see tears forming in her eyes.

"He had to go away for a little bit, sweetie," she replied.

"When is he coming back?"

"I don't know, sweetie. Fix up something to eat for yourself."

I stood up without hesitation. I walked over to the cabinet and got some juice and crackers. Using a chair, I climbed up to where we kept the plates and got out two. Then, I took out two wooden cups. I walked back over to the table and put the crackers on both plates and pushed one over to my mom. Then, very carefully, I poured some juice into both of the cups. I pushed one over to my mom again.

"I don't want anything, sweetie," she said.

"But Mommy, you have to eat something," I replied.

"No, I'll be fine."

"Mommy, you haven't eaten anything since yesterday!" I said.

"I don't want it."

"I won't leave you alone until you eat it, Mom. I'll make you eat." It was a threat often used by my mother when I wouldn't eat. She smiled wryly.

"All right, just a few," she said. She put a cracker in her mouth and washed it down with some juice. I smiled back at her. I was worried about her.

"Come on! Don't you die on me, Flame!" a voice from far away told me. I looked up into the ceiling. Was Flame my name?

"Flame, wake up!" It was a different voice this time. The earth started shaking.

"Mommy, I'm scared! What's happening?" I asked my mother.

She smiled. "No matter where you are, your father and I will always love you," she replied. She started to fade.

"Mommy?" I asked. "Where are you going?" I sat up coughing. Water came out of my mouth and I coughed even harder. I thought I was about to throw up.

"What happened?" I asked.

"Well, after you fell in the water—"

"I didn't fall, I was dragged. I can swim; some creature grabbed me."

"Well, after that we tried to get you, but you were already too deep and we thought you were gone. But then about a minute later, a Merman pulled you up and out of the water and told us what to do to get the water out of your lungs. And we did what he said and here you are."

"Where is he?" I asked.

"Near the edge of the river. He can talk, you know." I walked over to the edge of the river. There was the Merman that saved me. He looked like a human from the torso up, but I saw that a little lower than his belly button, there was a tail growing. He had dark black hair and dazzling blue eyes. He looked about thirty-years-old.

"Did you rescue me?" I asked.

"Yes, I did." His voice was very kind.

"Thank you. What attacked me?"

"It's called a Girmine. They are underwater creatures that usually eat land creatures by pulling them down into the water and drowning them. You were lucky I saw you. I don't like it when they try to eat humans because I am a half human."

"Thank you," I repeated.

"You're welcome."

He was about to swim away, but then I quickly asked, "Do you have a stone piece I can have?"

"There are lots of stones in the river here, miss. Is there any way you could be more specific?" I went over to the satchel and took out the first stone piece.

"It looks like this."

"Which one of you is an animal?" asked the Merman.

"Me," said Manka. To demonstrate, he turned into a wolf for a moment and then turned back into a human.

"We have one of the three stone pieces. We were told that you have the other one in your river. We need it to free Manka."

"I see. Well, you will have to trade us something for the stone piece."

"What is it?"

"Because we are a people that cannot leave the water for too long, we cannot get to something we want very much. We wish to have a piece of the mountain that we live in. You must go up to the very front of the mountains and cut off a piece of it with something. If you bring it back within two days then we will give you the next stone piece."

"I'll go," volunteered Manka.

"Me, too," said Deso.

"You're cut up, you're not going anywhere," argued Manka.

"I can walk fine!" yelled Deso.

"How about me and Eric go and you stay here with Flame?" suggested Manka. "You're not going to get very far anyways, being all cut up."

"All right, I'll stay."

"Good. Let's go, Eric." The boys set off.

"Be careful getting up that slope!" I called after them.

"Well, good night. I can bring up some people to look after you so you can get good sleep," offered the Merman.

"That'd be great," I said. "Thanks." As soon as they came up, Deso and I got underneath the quilt and fell asleep.

CHAPTER 13

The sun woke us up early the next morning. When we got up, there was a basket next to us filled to the brim with fruits. We got up and started eating them.

"I wonder how they're doing with finding the piece of the mountain," I said to Deso.

"They're probably getting along fine. The only hard part would be getting up the slope," replied Deso. Later that day, we decided to explore where we were. Promising the merpeople we wouldn't stray too far, we walked into the woods.

"Do you think we'll ever have a day where we just do nothing?" asked Deso.

I laughed. "Highly doubtful," I replied. "How's your cut?"

"Good, thanks to you." We made marks on the trees so we could find our way back later.

"I wonder if they're okay," I said again.

"Hey, they'll be fine. The only thing they got to worry about is killing each other if they get into a fight. Although

Manka will probably win that fight, and I wouldn't mind so much if Eric didn't come back."

I stopped walking. "Why do you hate him so much?" I asked.

"I don't. Well, I mean, it's not that I hate him, I just don't like him."

"Why not?"

Deso shrugged. "I don't know. I just don't like him much. I kind of get this vibe from him that he has done something bad in the past."

"Yeah, 'cause you've been an angel these past few years haven't you?"

"I don't mean like stealing or anything—that's baby stuff. I mean like killing and stuff."

"I highly doubt it. Come on, the kids like thirteen," I replied.

"That doesn't mean he didn't do some bad stuff."

"Hey, remember, he was the one who found the path for us? He has helped us a bit."

"One good deed doesn't free someone if they've done a lifetime of bad." I looked at him.

"Hypocrite," I said.

He pushed me lightly and playfully. I pushed him back a little harder. He pushed me quite hard this time and I pretended that he pushed me really hard and fell.

"Ouch!" I said. Deso knelt right next to me.

"Oh, sorry, Flame. Ah, man, now I feel bad."

"Gotcha." I laughed and pushed him to the ground. I got up and started running, marking some trees with my knife as I flew past them, Deso running right behind me. He eventually caught up to me and tackled me. We started wrestling and I beat him. I pinned him and as much as he struggled, he couldn't get out of my grip.

"All right, all right, you win!" said Deso, realizing defeat. I got off of him and helped him up.

"Let's start heading back, they might be back. It only took us about a night to get to the river in the first place." We started walking back, following the marks on the trees. Soon we came back to the river where we camped out, but there was no sign of Manka or Eric.

"Guess we have to wait a little longer," Deso said.

I sighed. "I'm bored."

"Well what do you want to do?"

I shrugged. "I would go swimming but after yesterday...I don't think I'll go in the river for a little while."

"Good! What were you thinking anyway?" Deso scolded.

I laughed. "Someone's being protective. And anyways," I said before Deso could make a retort, "curiosity got the best of me."

"Well, it almost cost you your life didn't it?"

"Well, I learned something new." I smiled widely at Deso. "If there's something swimming in the water, grab a spear with you before you go check it out. If it grabs you and pulls you into the water stab it."

Deso laughed. "Good lesson."

A couple of hours later, Manka and Eric came stumbling back. I ran up to Manka and hugged him.

"Whoa, no hug for me?" asked Eric.

"Um…I don't really know you that well…" I said. I awkwardly walked away.

"Did you get it?" asked Deso. Eric pulled a palm-sized rock out of his pocket.

The merman that pulled me out of the water came up out of it again.

"Did you get it?" he asked. Eric showed him the rock.

"Amazing," gasped the merman. He dived in the water for a moment and emerged holding the second stone piece.

Eric traded with the merman. One stone for another.

"Thank you so much!" I said.

"No. Thank you." The merman said.

"Do you know a way to get into the Erkon Kingdom?" I asked. "It's our next destination."

"Keep following the trail and in no time you'll find yourself where the Erkon Kingdom is."

"Thanks." The merman plunged back into the water.

"Let's start moving," said Manka.

"You just got back. Don't you want to rest?" asked Deso.

"Nah. Let's go."

We picked up our stuff and started to walk again.

CHAPTER 14

We kept to the path like the merman told us to do. When night started to fall, we gathered up some stones and twigs, took some matches Deso had cleverly stolen, and lit a fire. While the others slept, I decided to keep first watch. I sat a little bit away from the fire and wrapped myself in the quilt Mama Menny gave us. After about a half-hour of me keeping watch, I heard quiet footsteps behind me, and then someone sat next to me.

"Can't sleep?" I asked Eric.

"Kind of cold," he said, wrapping his arms around himself. I stood up, took the quilt off myself, and wrapped it around Eric's shoulders.

"I'll be fine," he said, trying to take it off and give it back to me.

"Keep it," I told him. "I don't need it."

We sat in silence for a few minutes.

"How come Deso doesn't like me?" he asked.

"I'm not really sure. He said he thought you did stuff that was bad. Can I ask you something?" Eric nodded. "The day you were in Mama Menny's house with us, I know you were running away from something. What was it?"

Eric hesitated before telling me. "Pirates." He said.

"You got involved with pirates?" I asked.

"I am a pirate. Or was a pirate." He sighed. "I don't even know anymore."

"So why'd you run away?"

"Listen, when you're a pirate, there's a code to keep to. I almost got hanged because half of us got caught by a fool on our ship. The other half went and rescued me. While we were camping, the other men fell asleep and I stayed awake. I decided to run away because the hangman's noose scared me. I accidently hit one of the men and he woke up and noticed I was trying to run away. If you run away when you're branded as a pirate you're either marooned or dead. I ran into the town and I saw people dancing and thought I could lose them in the crowd of people. That's when I asked you to dance. I had to leave because I saw one of the pirates close to where we were and was afraid they would find me. And they did, so I ran.

"They had to chase after me. And I ran really fast and hard back into the woods where I lost them again and spent the night in a tree. In the morning, they cornered my tree, so I jumped trees and started running again. Then I saw a cottage home. I started to knock on the door and Mama

Menny let me in. I needed to get away for a while because if they found me anywhere in the Arona Kingdom, they would kill me. Across the desert would be the best place for me. So I went with you guys."

"How'd they get you out of being hanged?" I asked.

"In the jail where they keep you before you hang, there are not a lot of guards. Shoot, two kids like us could overpower them if they knew how to fight. But anyways, once you get past the guards, the rest is kind of easy. The keys hang on a hook on a wall across from the cages they keep the prisoners in. You take them and unlock the door to the cage you're in. Now, the tricky part was getting out. What they did was they grabbed a pair of handcuffs and put them around my wrists, but they also grabbed the key. They made it seem like they were carrying me out like I was proven innocent. Once we got a little bit out of the range of the jail, they undid the handcuffs and we ran."

"Smart," I said. Eric nodded. I yawned.

"Why don't you go to sleep for a little while? I'll keep watch," said Eric.

"Yeah, all right." I got up and started walking toward the fire.

"Hey, Flame?" Eric asked.

"Yeah?" I turned around and Eric was right in front of me. He started to lean in toward me, but I turned my face sideways and his lips brushed my cheek. He turned away from me and walked back to the spot we were sitting at before. I put my hand on the place where he kissed me. Did I like him like that? I didn't even know. I walked over to the fire. Manka's eyes were open but shut tight when he saw I was looking at him.

"How much of that did you see?" I asked. He let out a small whine. I didn't know what it meant, but he probably saw more then he needed to. I inched closer to the fire. I tucked my arm under my head and fell asleep. The bright sun woke me up the next morning. I groaned and put my arms over my head, wanting more sleep. A cold nose nudged me on my side.

"Manka stop," I whined.

"Come on, Flame, we got to get going," said Deso.

I groaned. "Five more minutes," I begged. I felt someone's arms around my ankles. Deso started dragging me across the ground.

"All right, all right, I'm up!" I said. Deso dropped my ankles and I stood up. We took our things once more and started to walk. We mostly walked in silence, still trying to wake up. By the time the sun was right above us, we were starting to get really hungry. I looked in the satchel for something to eat. There was nothing there.

"What do you mean there's nothing there?" asked Deso.

"The spirit did say she could only supply unlimited food and water as long as we were in the desert," I replied. I sighed and closed the flap to the satchel.

Manka turned back into a human. "Well then, we better keep walking," he said. He stayed a human as we walked. He pulled Deso over to him and whispered something in his ear. Deso looked at Manka, his eyes wide. Manka whispered something else in Deso's ear. Deso nodded and Manka turned back into a wolf. It probably had to do with something that happened last night. I did not have a good feeling about this. We walked in silence until night fell once more. Well—almost complete silence, our stomachs refused to give up on begging for food.

When we stopped at night, we made another fire. Manka said he would take first watch. Deso, Eric, and I lay down closely to the fire and slept. I was almost asleep when I heard something close to me stir. A breath of wind passed by me. Deso had gotten up for some reason. I thought it was because he couldn't sleep, so I tried to sleep. Then, I heard whispering.

"Let's go," said Deso. I could hear two pairs of feet walking by me very silently. They went over to the side of where Eric was sleeping. I heard a soft thud and then Manka said, "Get up." A small groan from Eric rang in the air. I opened my eyes a little so I could see what they were doing. Manka and Deso were standing around Eric, who just got up looking confused.

"Is it time to go already?" he asked loudly.

"Shh!" said Deso. "And no, not yet, we just wanted to talk to you for a second."

"I saw you tried to kiss Flame last night," Manka said, "and let me tell you something, she is like a sister to me." Deso cracked his fingers menacingly.

"If you do anything to hurt her, or if you do anything to make her think you love her and then you abandon her, we will come after you and we will kill you," said Deso—his voice was shaking with anger. Eric chuckled.

"What's so funny?" asked Manka.

"If you really think I'm going to try something else after she wouldn't kiss me, you're wrong. I don't know what I was thinking, she's not even that pretty," Eric spat. Deso kicked him in his side.

"Consider yourself lucky she even talks to you," Deso said—his voice was filled with a cold hate I had never heard before. The both of them walked away. Eric looked over at me and I closed my eyes, pretending to be asleep. A couple of minutes after that I really did fall asleep. But it seemed like one minute later, I was woken up. The night was still young and we continued walking, our stomachs still complaining of the lack of food. Soon enough, the mountains on either side of us started to fade a little bit and grass started to come more into view. Even sooner, the shape of a gigantic castle started to form before our eyes.

"Guys, look at that," I said. "We're almost there!" We started to pick up our pace a little bit. The castle seemed close, but we kept walking until it was morning. It was getting close to noon by the time we were in front of the gates to the kingdom.

"So what happens now?" I asked. "I mean, we don't really know how long Manka's got to be a human right?"

"Well, there's obviously a forest because Mama Menny said something about a forest where her cousin lives. Let's have Manka turn into a human and we can find a forest or a ride and we'll go to her cousin." Manka turned back into a human. We walked toward the gates, which were glazed in gold and reached toward the sky.

"Who goes there?" asked a guard, standing on a pillar as high as the gate.

"Four children," I answered.

"What is your purpose here?"

"Our mother sent us to pick berries, but we couldn't find any so we have come back to her," I replied.

"Enter," said the guard. He waved his hand and the gate started to open and we walked right in.

We started walking to the town's square, which reminded me of the one in the Arona Kingdom. The ground was paved with snow white stones and the street bustled with activity. There were stores everywhere and huge lines for everything. We were walking along when we finally noticed the huge castle.

"Remember that Mama Menny said that her cousin lived at about the exact same place she does? Look, there's the castle and Mama Menny lives behind the castle so her cousin must live there too!"

"Did you say Mama Menny?" asked a voice behind me. I turned around. An old black man stood in front of me. He wore a long orange shirt that was decorated in bright patterns, and his pants matched. Under one arm he carried a basket filled with food, which made my mouth water, and under the other he had a very large bucket of water. His bushy eyebrows were up in surprise and his chocolate-colored eyes showed kindness.

"Yes," I said, "do you know her?"

"Of course!" he exclaimed. "She is my cousin!"

"We were sent to find you. You see, my friend here is a wolf and we need the last stone piece to bring him back to normal," I explained.

"Of course! Follow me!" he said.

CHAPTER 15

He ushered us into his house. Manka let out a painful groan and turned back into a wolf automatically.

"Sit, sit," said Mama Menny's cousin. "Are you hungry or thirsty?" he asked. He had seen me looking at the basket of food. The four of us nodded. "Go on and help yourselves. I'll make some tea." We reached into the basket gratefully and started to eat. I put some bread on the floor for Manka to eat.

"So tell me your story," said Mama Menny's cousin. I started to tell him how we wound up here between bites of food and help from Deso and Eric. It seemed like it took forever to tell, but it was finally finished. Mama Menny's cousin sat there the whole time, his eyes wide, listening intently, never interrupting.

"So you need the stone piece, yes?" he asked.

"It would help us a lot," I replied. "I can't stand seeing Manka being a human for only an hour a day, and I don't think he likes it very much."

"I see. One minute." He got up from the table and started looking through everything in his house, which caused it to be very loud inside the small space we were in.

"Aha!" he exclaimed. He emerged from somewhere deep inside the rubble and a glass case was in his hand. In it, the ruby red stone piece rested.

"Oh my gosh, thank you so much!" I said.

"Anything to help out a daughter of Rosanne," he replied.

I stopped smiling. "How do you know my mother's name?" I asked.

"She and I were very good friends. And so were your father and I. You look just like her, and your father, of course. But you have both their hair."

"What do you mean?" I asked.

"Your mother had fine, brown, silky hair, and your father's hair was as golden as the sun. Your hair is a mix of those two."

"Golden brown," I whispered, wrapping some hair around my finger.

He smiled. "Exactly." He opened the case and gave me the last stone piece. "As soon as you put those together, it will take all four of you back to Mama Menny's house together."

"I'm not going back," said Eric. "I have to stay here." He looked at me and I nodded. I could understand why he had to stay.

"So…good-bye," said Deso, somewhat cheerfully.

"Bye. It has been fun being on this trip with you three."
He came close to me and kissed me on the check again.
"Take care," he whispered in my ear. "I know I'll see you
again someday."

I waved. "Good-bye!" I said. He went out the door.

I took the two stone pieces out of the satchel and placed
them on the table. I took the third one and put the three of
them together. The whole table started to shake, and very
quickly after, the whole cottage. I grabbed onto Manka and
Deso. Suddenly, a blinding white flash went through the
air and I felt the air spinning around me, making me spin,
along with Manka and Deso.

When the spinning stopped, I opened my eyes. There,
in front of me, sat Mama Menny's cottage.

CHAPTER 16

I felt something in my hand—a cool stone rested in it. I opened my hand and there were the three stone pieces, finally joined as one. Manka was still a wolf, though. I knocked on the door to the cottage. Mama Menny stood in front of me, smiling widely.

"You made it!" she exclaimed. She laughed happily. "Come on, come in!" We walked inside her house. I could hardly believe it was almost over.

"Give me the stone!" exclaimed Mama Menny. I handed it over to her. She ran her thumb over it, as if she could hardly believe we brought it to her.

"Amazing," she whispered. "I thought I would never see this again."

"Again?" I asked. "What do you mean 'again'?"

"Well, usually I would just read the spell to the people who had been turned into animals, but then Salma found out and she sought out to destroy it. Lucky for you, it is indestructible and it cracked and flew into those three places you went to find it. Lucky for me, when it flew into the Erkon Kingdom, my cousin, Abdul, found it, recognized it, and kept it safe."

"So can you read what it says on the back?" asked Deso. "We need Manka back."

"Yes, of course!" Mama Menny put her glasses on. She started to chant what it said on the back, and it sounded like a very ancient language. She chanted for about a minute and then stopped. Exactly at the time when she stopped, a gold flash came out from Manka. I couldn't see what was happening to him and I ended up closing my eyes because it was so bright. When the flash was gone, Manka stood in front of me, completely human.

"Just so you know, you can still turn back into a wolf anytime you want," said Mama Menny.

"Really?" asked Manka. "And I won't be stuck like that forever or only be able to be a human for an hour each day?" Mama Menny shook her head.

"Thank you so much," I said.

She stroked my hair. "Anytime, child," she replied. "And come visit me sometime."

I hugged Manka. I put my hands around his and Deso's shoulders. The three of us walked out of Mama Menny's cottage and back into the woods.